# Let's Clean Up!

Peggy Perry Anderson

HOUGHTON MIFFLIN COMPANY  BOSTON
WALTER LORRAINE *wL* BOOKS

To my dear sister Linda,
whose housecleaning habits
forced me to ask for my own room.

Walter Lorraine (wr) Books

Copyright © 2002 by Peggy Perry Anderson
All rights reserved. For information about permission to
reproduce selections from this book, write to Permissions,
Houghton Mifflin Company, 215 Park Avenue South,
New York, New York 10003.

www.houghtonmifflinbooks.com

*Library of Congress Cataloging-in-Publication Data*
Anderson, Peggy Perry.
    Let's clean up! / by Peggy Perry Anderson
        p.    cm.
    Summary: When Joe messes up his room immediately
after his mother has cleaned it, his method of straightening
it up again does not meet with her approval.
    RNF ISBN 0-618-19602-1        PA ISBN 0-618-55523-4
    [1. Orderliness—Fiction. 2. Cleanliness—Fiction. 3.
Frogs—Fiction. 4. Stories in rhyme.]
    I. Title.
    PZ8.3.A5484 Le 2002
    [E]—dc21                                      2001039612

ISBN–13: 978-0-618-55523-9

Printed in Singapore
TWP 10 9 8 7 6 5 4 3 2

Mother said,
"I have the broom.
Let's clean up
this messy room."

Mother cleaned high.

Mother cleaned low.

# Mother cleaned the room for Joe.

"I have room to ride my train."

"I have room to fly my planes."

"I can race my racing cars."

"And launch my rocket to the stars."

"There's room to bounce upon my bed."

"Or room to hide below instead."

"I can build a tent today."

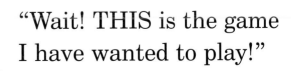

"Wait! THIS is the game
I have wanted to play!"

"What will I find inside the toy box?"

"Oh boy! Here are all of my building blocks!"

"I'll build a tower to the sky!"

It was then
that Mother
began to cry.

"Don't worry, Mom. I have the broom."

"I'll clean up this messy room!"

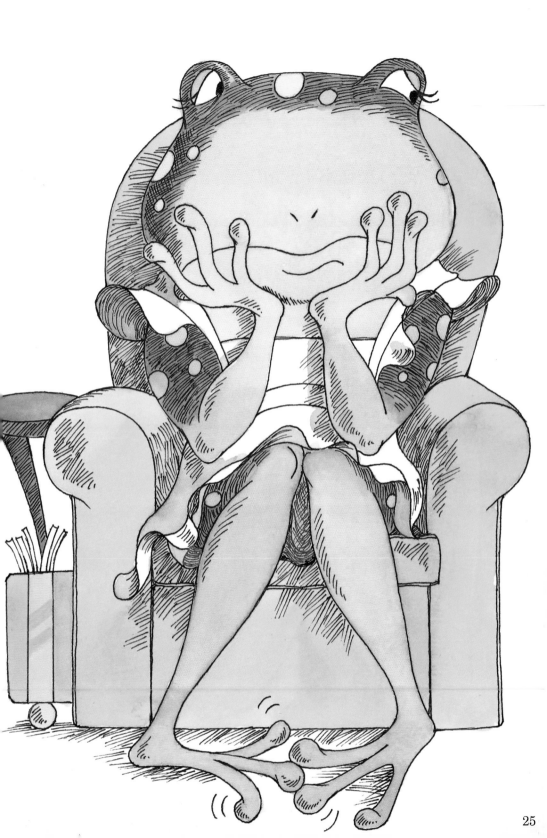

"My," said Mother, "you cleaned in a hurry."

"I told you, Mother,
not to worry!"

"Oh, Mother, look and see."

"My room is as
clean as it can be."

"Oh, Joe, you worked so hard."

"Now what shall we do about the yard?"

Joe said,
"Mom you're right.
It's true.
To really clean
UP it takes
two!"